1

LONER LIFE IN ANOTHER WORLD

CONTENTS

Ch. 01	I Bet You're Wondering How I Got Here	001
Ch. 02	I Went to Another World and All I Got Was This Crappy Skillset	019
Ch. 03	When Did This Shift to the Survival Genre?	031
Ch. 04	This World's a Piece of Cake	045
Ch. 05	My Loner Life Is in Dire Peril!	057
Ch. 06	The Power of the Nerds	069
Ch. 07	Been a Long Time Since I Held a Conversation	079
Ch. 08	What's With All These Exclamation Marks!!!	093
Ch. 09	The Class Rep's Spectacular Comedy Routine	105
Ch. 10	The Fundamentals of Life, Emphasis on "Fun"	117
Ch. 11	If I Had Just One Last Wish, I Would Like a Tasty Fish	129
Ch. 12	The Loner Life Chose Me, so Let Me Live It	141
EXTRA BONUS STORY	The Forest Is Dark, so Just Cut a Path Through All the Monsters!	157

RIGHT NOW...

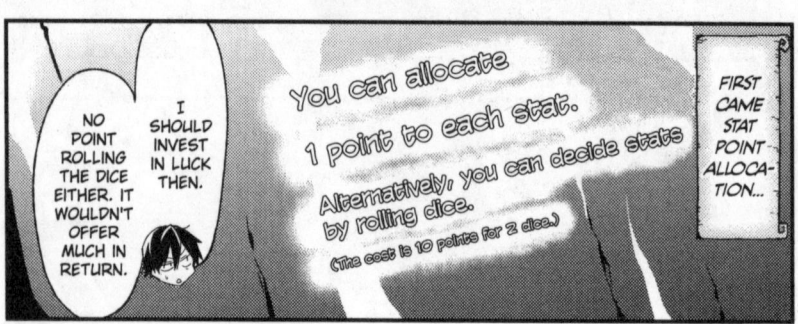
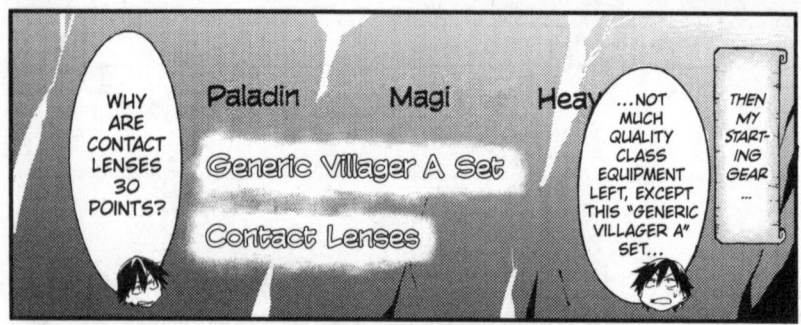

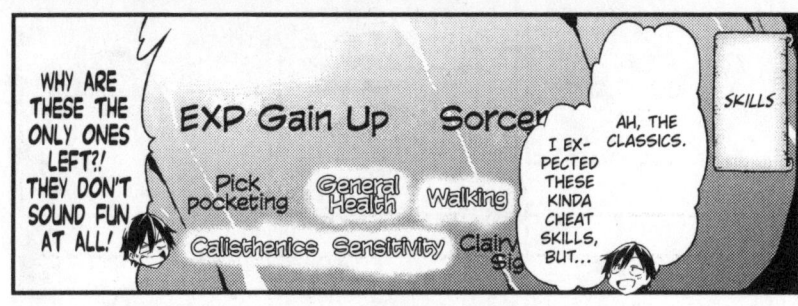
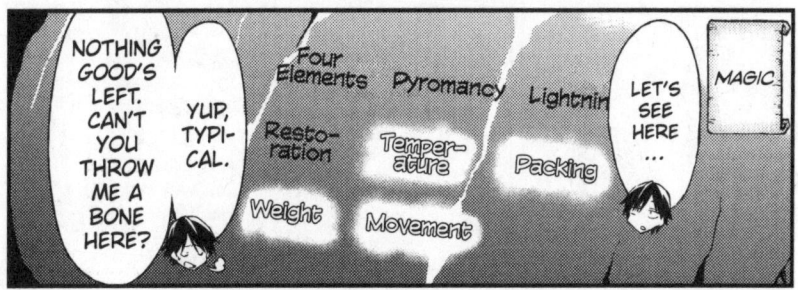

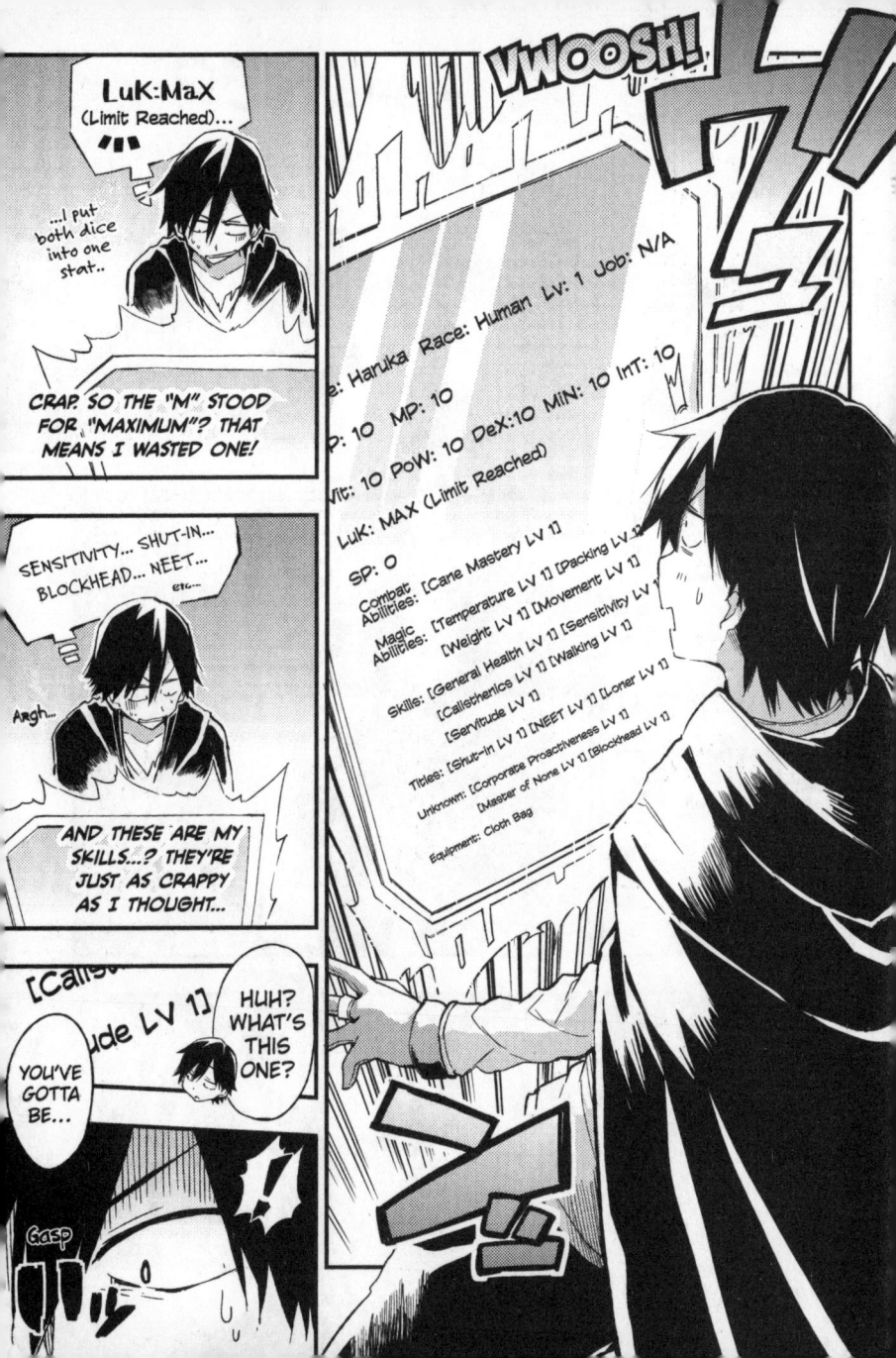

Plopshroom
Edible. Draws out latent abilities.

...A CAVERN?

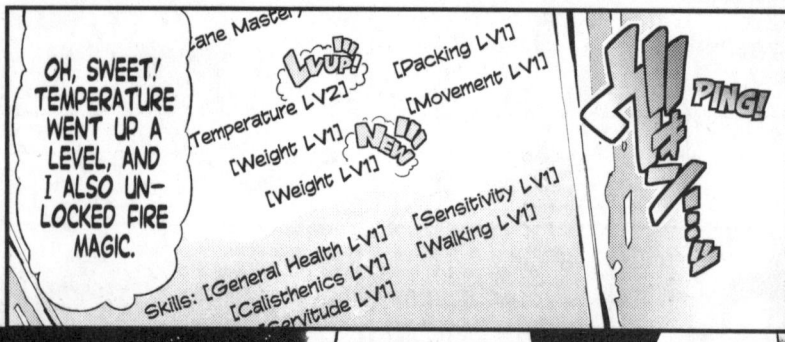

FWIP

GASP

DAY 2

MORNING, HUH? LOOKS LIKE I MADE IT THROUGH THE NIGHT.

phew!

GLANCE GLANCE

MAN I'M HUNGRY...

GROWL...

...

Ghh...

GUESS I HAVE THOSE ITEMS TO THANK, ALONG WITH MY SHUT-IN SKILL.

I FIGURED BEING A SOCIAL RECLUSE WOULD HAVE ITS PERKS!

『Shut-in:
【 A man's home is his castle. Your living space is extra-safe. 】』

LET'S USE THAT FIRE MAGIC I LEARNED YESTERDAY.

CLATTER

Fire Magic

I CAN USE THOSE MUSHROOMS I GOT, AND SOME OF THAT JERKY I FOUND IN MY BAG.

NOW A LITTLE SEASONING AND SIMMERING...

shh... shh...

VOILA

AND THAT'S BREAKFAST, BABY!

DAMN, STUFF'S NOT HALF BAD!

Yummy

SHINE

NOM

...DO VILLAGERS REALLY USE THIS KINDA GEAR THOUGH?

La-di-daah...

SEEMS WAY MORE LIKE A "GENERIC SURVIVALIST A" SET TO ME.

I CAN'T BELIEVE IT CAME WITH KITCHENWARE.

THIS "GENERIC VILLAGER SET A" SURE IS USEFUL.

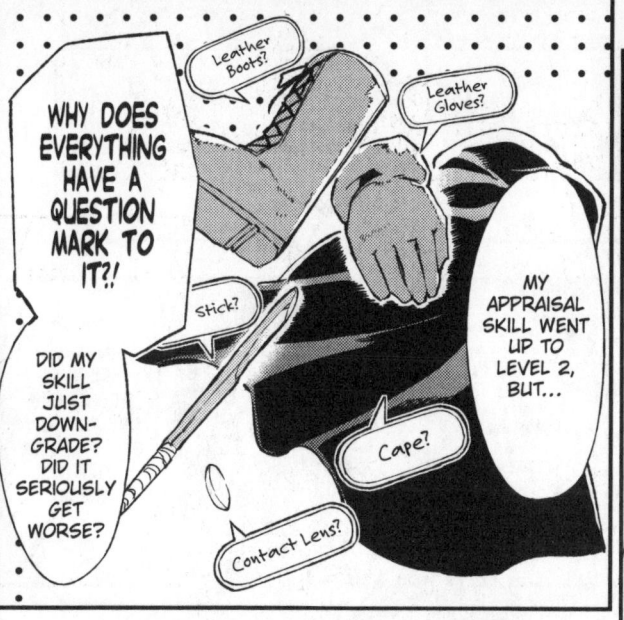

Shimmer

Success
...I'D MASTERED THE ART OF ONE-SHOTTING GOBLINS!

-DA-DUN!

Gorgeous
I WAS ALSO ABLE TO CRAFT SOME LOVELY FURNITURE FOR MY HOME BASE.

WITH ALL THAT TAKEN CARE OF...

Rooogh!!!

THINGS ARE GOING PRETTY WELL FOR ME... I MIGHT NOT BE SO DOOMED AFTER ALL.

Oh yeah, it's all coming together.

SZUU-SNATCH!

"YOU'RE MINE!"

DASH DASH DASH *GRRRR!!*

"GET IN MY BELLY, SCRAP MEAT!"

heh *heh heh heh*

SCREECH!!

"I YEARN FOR FLEEESH!!!"

DASH DASH

"...WAIT. IS SOMETHING NEARBY? A GOB? NO... SOMETHING ELSE?"

GLARE

Presence Detection, go.

I'm outta here!

"GET BACK HERE! I JUST WANNA EAT YOOOU!"

IT'S SOME OF MY CLASSMATES...

FWOOSH

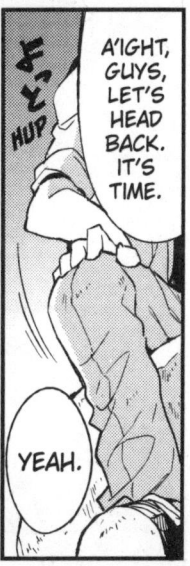

THANKS FOR THE ASSIST!

HECK YEAH!

This is awkward...

Well, uh...

SO, I...UH... HM. YOU GUYS ALL RIGHT? WHY'RE YOU OUT HERE SO LATE?

GUESS I SHOULD START WITH SMALL TALK...

AW, CRAP, IT'S BEEN SO LONG, I FORGOT HOW TO TALK TO PEOPLE...

sweat

AH, UH... NO, IT'S FINE...

NO BIGGIE, EHEH...? YEAH, NO BIG...

WE'RE ON THE RUN...

YOU'RE WHAT?!

!!! DA-DUN!

YOU GUESSED IT: THE NERDS.

THEIR FIGHT ROUSED THE JOCKS INTO ACTION AS WELL, PUSHING THE ENEMIES BACK EVEN MORE.

HAAAH!!!

THRUST! もくもくもく SILENCE
FWOOSH!

ISN'T IT SCARY TO FIGHT SO QUIETLY?! YOU COULDA GRUNTED OR SOMETHING!

THEY WORDLESSLY FOUGHT OFF THE GOBLIN HORDE.

GWOOSH!
CLASH!!

MUTTER MUTTER

THEY'D BEEN DOING SOME SERIOUS SURVIVAL TRAINING JUST FOR THIS KINDA SCENARIO.

IT MIGHT HAVE BEEN USELESS IN OUR WORLD, BUT HERE...

THE NERDS MADE CAMP AND STARTED A FIRE TO COOK AND KEEP WARM.

RUSTLE

THE CLASS REP SNAPPED BACK TO HER SENSES AND LED EVERYONE TO A SAFE AREA BY THE RIVER.

AT LEAST NOBODY GOT HURT...

BUT IT DIDN'T LAST LONG...

This is so lame. For reals.

I don't, like, wanna put up tents and stuff.

HOW COME WE GOTTA DO THIS STUFF?

THIS KINDA WORK IS FOR THE GUYS, NOT US.

NAH, I WANT OUT.

PLEASE WAIT!

SERIOUSLY?! EVEN I'VE WORKED HARDER THAN THOSE CLOWNS!

So lame...

Gee, it sure is boring around here...

SOME OF THE STUDENTS STILL HELPED THE CLASS REP OUT, BUT A GOOD CHUNK JUST LAZED AROUND.

IN THE END, ALL THE GROUP TASKS GOT PAWNED OFF TO THE NERDS.

HUFF PUFF...?

YOU GUYS ARE ON TOP OF IT!

DESPITE EVERYTHING, THE NERDS CONTINUED TO DILIGENTLY FEND OFF THE MONSTERS.

HOW'D YOU FIND THAT OUT?

Geheheh...

MESMERIZE

THEY TOOK THEM AT THE START.

SO YOU WERE LEVELING UP TO DEFEND AGAINST THEM AT SOME POINT? GOTCHA.

PUPPETRY

THEY DID THIS BECAUSE THEY'D LEARNED THAT SOME OF THE OTHERS CHOSE SKILLS CALLED PUPPETRY AND MESMERIZE. THESE ALLOWED THE USERS TO BEND OTHERS TO THEIR WILL.

EVENTUALLY, THE BASE CAMP LAID BEFORE ME.

whoosh...

ouchie... why'd he have to bite my hand...

IT HURT A BIT, BUT I STILL PRESSED ONWARD.

FWOOO...

ALL THESE TATTERED TENTS AND WRECKED FENCES...

I GUESS NO ONE WOULD'VE KNOWN HOW TO FIX ALL THIS UP WITHOUT THE NERDS AROUND.

NO-BODY'S HERE...

DID THEY SET UP A NEW CAMP ELSE-WHERE?

OH? WHAT'S THIS?

I WONDER WHERE THEY ARE...

BUT THAT'S NOT WHAT THE NERDS SAID...

Enemy Tracking Skill

ALL RIGHT THEN. I'LL JUST FOLLOW THESE TRACKS.

Clairvoyant Sight

HALT

...FOUND SOMETHING.

STEP STEP STEP

DASH DASH DASH

STEP STEP STEP STEP

HUH...? SOMETHING'S COMING THIS WAY...

THIS LOOKS FAMILIAR...

STARE

CHATTER CHATTER

OH, MAN LOOK AT THE TIME...

I SHOULD GET BACK HOME AND GET DINNER STARTED...

SWISH

YEAH, THINK I'LL FRY UP SOME CHICKEN TODAY...

RUSTLE RUSTLE

HOLD IT RIGHT THERE.

PLEASE, CAN YOU, LIKE, TOTALLY TEACH US HOW TO SURVIVE AND STUFF?!

PRETTY PLEASE!!! WE NEED TO REACH THEM AND SAY SORRY!!!

PLEASE!!!

DA-DUN!

UH... O-OKAY?

WHAT THE HELL JUST HAPPENED?!

FLAP FLAP FLAP

BIMBOS SUCCESSFULLY INDENTURED.

Servant List
Head Bimbo
Bimbo A
Bimbo B
Bimbo C
Bimbo D

AW, CRAP, DID I JUST AGREE TO HELP THEM?!

SHING

SKILL ACTIVATING...

TH-THAT'S NOT MY REAL NAME!

GOODNESS GRACIOUS...

HUH?

IT CAN'T BE...

HEY THERE!

CLASS REP...?

WHY ARE YOU CALLING ME BY THAT?! WE'VE KNOWN EACH OTHER SINCE THE FIRST GRADE!

OH, CRAP... HOW DO I EVEN EXPLAIN THIS...

I'D LIKE AN EXPLANATION MYSELF!

URP

They look a little funny...

ANYWAY... HARUKA, DID SOMETHING HAPPEN TO SHIMAZAKI AND HER FRIENDS?

WHY ARE YOU HANGING OUT WITH THEM ANYWAY?

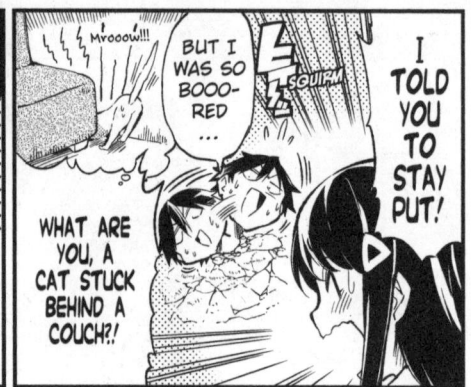

THANK YOU SO MUCH.

YOU WERE JUST TRYING TO HELP, RIGHT?

AND OTA'S GROUP TOO.

THIS IS KINDA TAKING A WHILE, SO... CAN I GO HOME NOW?

HEH...

H-HEY! WE'RE PUTTING OUR HEARTS ON OUR SLEEVES HERE!

THIS ONLY TOOK SO LONG BECAUSE YOU WOULDN'T EXPLAIN IT YOURSELF!

Wait... go home...?

WHAT DO YOU MEAN BY "HOME"?

DO YOU HAVE A PLACE NEARBY?

HUH?	WHAT ELSE WOULD I MEAN? I BUILT A HOUSE.

YOU CAN'T JUST UNDERTAKE SOMETHING LIKE THAT IN YOUR SPARE TIME!!!

N-NO... I JUST MADE IT IN MY FREE TIME.

WHAAAT?!

CREEP *FLAP* *FLAP* *GYAAAH!!! GYAAAH!!!*

HOW DID YOU DO THAT ALREADY?! WERE YOU BORN HERE OR SOMETHING?!

UMM... HOW MANY PEOPLE CAN FIT IN YOUR HOUSE...?

WHISPER WHISPER WHISPER

WHISTLE!!

...NO BOYS ALLOWED, HUH?

OH HECK YEAH! I EVEN LEARNED THE LIGHTNING MAGIC SKILL!

[Lightning Magic LV 1]

SKLUGE!

I GOT ONE!

VIC- TORY!

DA-DAAAH!

HEHEHEH...

HOW DID YOU DO THAT?

You used my spell?

H-Huh?

I JUST LEARNED FROM WHAT I SAW.

Packing

『Packing』
【Packs up things using magic. Works on anything!】

WAIT, YOU CAN USE THAT TO LEARN MAGIC?! THAT'S CHEATING!

Go!

Packing!

I LEARNED IT BY WRAPPING THE SPELL UP WITH MY PACKING SKILL.

OR, SOME- THING LIKE THAT...

IF YOU COULD TELL ME, STARTING ON THE RIGHT...

...I NEED TO KNOW YOUR CURRENT LEVELS.

AHEM

BEFORE WE GET TO GRINDING THOUGH...

I THINK I'M 21...

YEP.

I'M AT 20.

UMM... 16?

YEP!

17 HERE.

I'M LEVEL 19.

I'M ONLY LEVEL 7...

Why was I getting so excited earlier...?

Ya-hoo!

Lv16

WAIT, THE LOWEST IS LEVEL 16?!

HOW'D THEY GET THAT HIGH ALREADY?!

HUH?

YOU'VE GOTTA BE KIDDING ME!

YOU FOUGHT WELL, KOBOLD. WE WON'T LOSE THE NEXT ENCOUNTER EITHER.

TIME FOR US TO MAKE OUR WAY THROUGH THE FOREST...

...AND PRESS ON TO THAT TOWN I KEEP HEARING ABOUT.

Wahoo! We did it! Those kobolds were kinda cute, don't you think? Can we keep them?!

GUESS IT'S ABOUT THAT TIME...

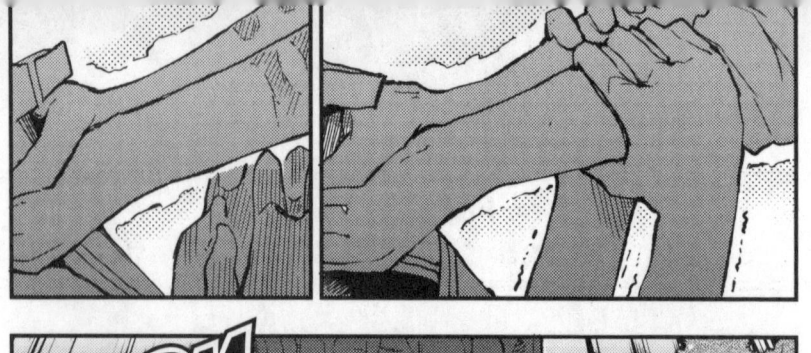

To be continued...

The Forest is Dark,
so Just Cut a Path Through All the Monsters!

The forest was a dark territory fraught with despair, its thick foliage hiding nothing but strife for all who dared trespass. This other world was a place filled with terrifying monsters, frightening danger, and unending sorrow. How many times had I woken up at night cowering? How often had I asked the universe, "What did I do to deserve this?" People who are plunged into despair and fear don't dream; there simply isn't a place to store dreams or hope in a place like this. Being forced to smile and pretend everything was okay, one couldn't do anything but put on a brave face and try to subsist...survive as best as they could. Throwing hope away, the only thing holding one together was the fear of death, and the faint idea that all of this might be one huge mistake. No one wanted to end up in this hopeless, sad world in the first place...

That was exactly why I spent my days enjoying the luxurious bath I'd installed in my cave. It was why I'd been eating an assortment of gourmet mushrooms and drinking such sweet, sweet juice. It was almost criminal how relaxed I was living. Indeed, if life were so scary and cruel, then it was society's fault that I had to cope as such...

The next morning, when I had gone out to take a look around the forest, it was the first time I saw this world's scenery as something beautiful. The way the sunlight poured in from the gaps between the leaves like a rain of gold was truly something to behold. The brilliant sparkle of the river was also quite the sight.

Perhaps it had something to do with the beautiful decoration of the cavern, or the delicious mushroom dishes I'd been eating. Or maybe it was because I was sharing my home base with my classmates. After they bathed themselves to their heart's content in my unnecessarily fancy bathroom, their fear all seemed to dissipate, and they managed to get a good night's sleep. After all the crying, the nightmares, and the fear subsided, perhaps they'd be able to see this world in a different light. After we'd formed a routine and began finding some normality in our lives here, we almost felt stupid for being so afraid in the beginning...

"We don't really need to attack the monsters, do we?"

"They'll come after us if we don't!"

"That's why we'll blindside them. That way we can all sleep easy at night. It'll make for a more secure environment where none of us have to be afraid of being attacked by surprise."

"That's just a massacre!"

"No no, it'll be more dangerous if we're attacked first, right?"

"You're the dangerous one here, talking about taking them by surprise!"

Gathering our courage and masking our fear, we decided to take on a weak enough monster for our current levels...but in the end, the monster was able to fend us off.

"That's what you get for skipping gym class back home. Even if you don't win by force, you can still win if you know what to do, remember?"

"Huh?"

"Didn't I tell you before? Just get behind them and scream at the top of your lungs. That'll scare them off...probably..."

"Not everyone can scream with that creepy tone of yours! That'd scare off anyone, not just monsters!"

In between the spare time we had from gathering mushrooms, they would hunt monsters, raising their levels in the process. And they got pretty used to it...

"Like, yeah! If we sneak in on them from behind and beat 'em to death, then we can also gang on up them when they're down, just to make sure, y'know?"

Sneaking up on monsters, digging pitfalls for them to fall into, tangling them up with ropes made of ivy... even throwing sand in their eyes. The monsters were beginning to look more and more like the victims here.

"This isn't about winning or losing, but making sure they get a good beating...I guess?"

"It isn't about who's stronger or weaker, but winning...I think?"

Using their skills, they began beating the monsters to a pulp. But soon after, they started worrying about failure. It was good to see them use their skills more though. In the end, they were developing pretty cunning methods to kill off the monsters.

"So we sprinkle water on them and use electric magic to—"

"No way, if we use earth magic to create a slippery slope, then channel the electric current through the water, it'd be totes better!"

Talk about adapting to the situation... Their imaginations were running wild, coming up with so many colorful yet efficient ways to torture the monsters with traps... It was almost enough to make me feel sorry for the beasts out there. That dark and creepy forest frightened me enough, but after hearing the craziness spewing from the girls' mouths, it almost seemed tame.

"That's awful! That goblin hasn't even done anything!"

"It's not our fault though? It just walked forward and became immobilized?"

"Maybe it smelled the poison fumes coming from the toadstool mushroom trap we set..."

"That's still too mean... Even if you are fighting against them, that's way too extreme!"

The goblin in question was pretty damn weak, its level laughably low, and it wasn't even equipped with much besides dirty clothes and a wooden pole. Powerless and unable to move, it simply fell prey to the girls...all in the name of preventative safety.

"No, humans must fight with their wits. Succumbing to the monsters' level and waving around murder sticks is just barbaric. We must prepare ourselves to ensure our victory. If animals hunt with their claws and fangs, then we humans must use our brains to overcome obstacles! That's how it's supposed to work!"

"I understand that much, but you're basically dropping nukes on ants here!"

Still, their mad hunt persisted. Everyone had their fill of food, warmth, and (questionable) fun. The cave slowly became a place filled with merrymaking and laughter.

I loudly excused myself, saying it was too embarrassing having to live with so many women. I went outside, leaving my cozy cave behind. I didn't stray too far, avoiding the monsters as best as I could, and erected my tent successfully. I lit up some torches to keep the beasts at bay. Protecting the cave's entrance. Thanks to that, everyone was able to sleep well, slowly giving them the courage to conquer this new land. With everyone resting easy, they could forget about all those nights they cried themselves to sleep, and come to realize that this world was hiding some of its beauty. For the first time in a long while, we were able to look up at the night sky with a smile, the stars above giving us a faint twinkle of our long lost hope...

— ──────── **Episode end.** ──────── —

1
LONER LIFE IN ANOTHER WORLD
COMMENT

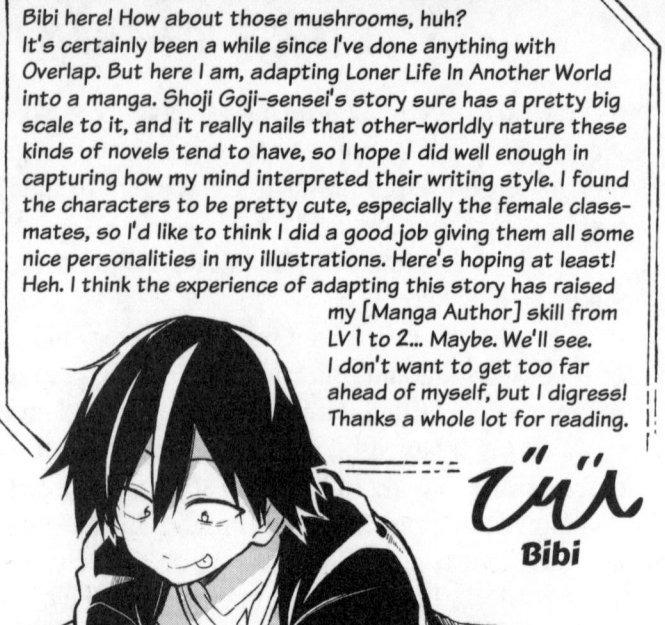

Bibi here! How about those mushrooms, huh? It's certainly been a while since I've done anything with Overlap. But here I am, adapting Loner Life In Another World into a manga. Shoji Goji-sensei's story sure has a pretty big scale to it, and it really nails that other-worldly nature these kinds of novels tend to have, so I hope I did well enough in capturing how my mind interpreted their writing style. I found the characters to be pretty cute, especially the female classmates, so I'd like to think I did a good job giving them all some nice personalities in my illustrations. Here's hoping at least! Heh. I think the experience of adapting this story has raised my [Manga Author] skill from LV 1 to 2... Maybe. We'll see. I don't want to get too far ahead of myself, but I digress! Thanks a whole lot for reading.

Bibi

Original Author: **Shoji Goji**

Thanks so much for buying and reading this volume. It really means a lot. I'm just happy that my story got a manga adaptation. I'm Shoji Goji. I'm what you'd refer to as the original author of this work. To be honest, when I was talking to the editorial staff at Comic Gardo about adapting my story into a manga, the general vibe was, "There's no way this could be adapted! It's a story that's pretty hard to visualize, you know?" I kind of threw it out of my head to begin with, so actually putting images to it just seemed so monumental. Honestly, I'm just thankful that Bibi-sama took up the job... I feel like I owe them an apology, almost (ahahahh...) I'm glad their name is more prominent than mine on this, because they've done a tremendous job expanding the setting and breathing life into it as a visual medium. I've really enjoyed seeing the world that they managed to draw based on how they interpreted my writing, and I hope you've all enjoyed that too. But honestly, that's all from me. Thank you so much for reading this, and I hope you continue to do so.

Loner Life in Another World

Original Story: Shoji Goji
Artist: Bibi

VOL. 1

HITORI BOCCHI NO ISEKAI KOURYAKU VOL. 1
© 2019 Bibi
© Shoji Goji/OVERLAP
First published in Japan in 2019 by OVERLAP, Inc.
English translation rights reserved by Kaiten Books, LLC.
Under license from OVERLAP, Inc., Tokyo JAPAN

No portion of this book may be reproduced, scanned, or translated in any form without written permission from the copyright holders. This is a work of fiction. Names, characters, places and events are products of the author's imagination, and any resemblances to actual events or places or persons, living or dead, is entirely coincidental.

For press inquiries or review copies, please send all correspondence to info@kaitenbooks.com

Kaiten Books and the Kaiten Books logo are copyright of Kaiten Books, LLC. All rights reserved

ISBNs: 978-1-952241-00-0 (paperback)
978-1-952241-01-7 (ebook)

Printed in Canada

First Printing: March 2020

Translation
Andrew Hodgson

Editing
Kris Swanson

Typesetting
Kazushi Mizutani

Retouch and Proofreading
Christian Knoll

Production Manager
Garrison Denim

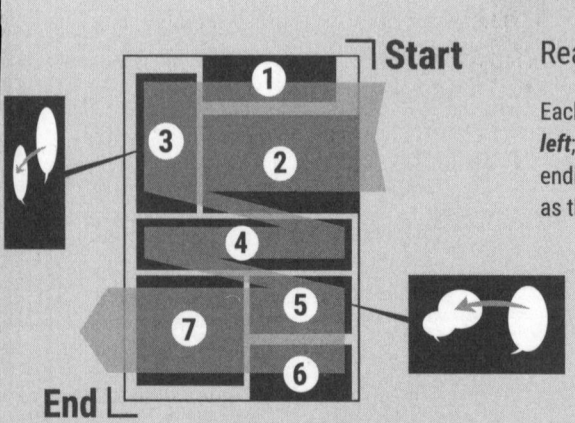

Reading Instructions:

Each page reads from *right to left*; starting from the top right, ending at bottom left. Simple as that. Follow diagram on left.

Come visit us online at: www.kaitenbooks.com